# Chapter One

"A gardening competition?" said Ben.

"No, no," said Mr Prewett. "It's a growing competition. I've got the seeds here. All you have to do is plant them."

Ben sighed. "I don't know anything about growing things."

"You don't know anything about anything."

Ben didn't know who had said it but everyone was laughing. Mr Prewett walked around the classroom putting the small, stripy seeds on each table. "Now, Class Four," he said. "Let's see if you can grow some monster sunflowers."

# You Can Do It, Stanley

Irena Green

*Illustrated by Susan Hellard*

www.kidsatrandomhouse.co.uk

*For all little seeds*

YOU CAN DO IT, STANLEY
A CORGI PUPS BOOK 0 552 55121 X

Published in Great Britain by Corgi Books,
an imprint of Random House Children's Books

This edition published 2004

1 3 5 7 9 10 8 6 4 2

Papers used by Random House Children's Books are natural,
recyclable products made from wood grown in sustainable forests.
The manufacturing processes conform to the environmental regulations
of the country of origin.

Set in Bembo Schoolbook by Palimpsest Book Production Limited,
Polmont, Stirlingshire

Corgi Books are published by Random House Children's Books,
61–63 Uxbridge Road, London W5 5SA,
a division of The Random House Group Ltd,
in Australia by Random House Australia (Pty) Ltd,
20 Alfred Street, Milsons Point, Sydney, NSW 2061, Australia,
in New Zealand by Random House New Zealand Ltd,
18 Poland Road, Glenfield, Auckland 10, New Zealand,
and in South Africa by Random House (Pty) Ltd,
Endulini, 5A Jubilee Road, Parktown 2193, South Africa

THE RANDOM HOUSE GROUP Limited Reg. No. 954009
www.kidsatrandomhouse.co.uk

A CIP catalogue record for this book
is available from the British Library.

Printed and bound in Great Britain by
Cox & Wyman Ltd, Reading, Berkshire

# Contents

Series Reading Consultant: Prue Goodwin,
Lecturer in Literacy and Children's Books,
University of Reading

It was true Ben didn't know
anything about growing seeds,
but he knew someone who
did.

"I'd talk to it," said Grandad.
"And give it a name."
"But . . ."
"How about Susan? That's a
nice name for a sunflower."

"That's a girl's name," said Ben.

"Stuart then, or Simon."

"I'm not calling it Stuart."

"Course," said Grandad. "You could call it Stanley."

"That's your name," said Ben.

Grandad searched his pockets and pulled out a pair of woolly gloves.

"And you could wear these," he

said. "My growing gloves."

"Do they work?"

"Put them on," said
Grandad. "Give them a try."

"All right," said Ben. "You'll
have to hold, um, Stanley."

Ben wasn't sure if it was the
growing gloves, or because he
had been holding the seed so

tightly, but when he put the gloves on, his fingers began to tingle. Carefully he filled a flowerpot with compost and dipped a woolly finger into the middle to make a hole.

Ben took the seed in the palm of his hand and closed his fingers around it. He held it up to his mouth and breathed

warm breath
on it. Ben
looked
around to
make sure
no one
was
listening.

"Do your
best, Stanley," he
whispered and dropped the
seed into the hole.

For a second Ben thought
about winning, but not for
long. He knew who was going
to win. It would be Jennifer,

Jennifer Sugden. She won
everything. She liked winning.
She liked it so much that it
was hard to be pleased for her
when she did.

But Ben didn't care about
winning. He had Stanley and just
trying to grow him into the biggest
sunflower was going to be fun.

"You all right in there?" said Ben, holding the pot up to his ear. "Warm enough?"

He looked at Grandad.

"Stanley's got the hump," he said. "He's not talking to me."

"Now," said Grandad, "I never said anything about conversation."

Ben took Stanley home and stood him on the windowsill.

"You thirsty?" he said, dribbling water into the pot.

Every day before he went to school, Ben made sure that Stanley was comfortable. "Bit more sun?" he said, opening the curtains a little further.

And then, at the end of the first week, Ben noticed something green in Stanley's pot. When he looked closer, he could see that the something green meant the end of Stanley Seed and the beginning of Stanley Sunflower.

"Brilliomo, Stan."

By the end of the next week Stanley was helping Ben learn

his tables. And by the end of another week Stanley had six leaves and was supporting United.

"Did you see that, Stan? It was a penalty for sure."

Now that Ben had got the hang of it, he talked to Stanley all the time. Stanley hadn't actually said anything back but Ben was sure that it was only a matter of time. He hoped it would be before Monday. Stanley had to go to school on Monday. He had to be measured and planted out.

# Chapter Two

"Now listen," said Ben, as they walked to school. "We're not going to win this. Jennifer'll

win. She'll have a huge
sunflower, with nice leaves and
a straight stem but it doesn't
matter. If you're littler than the
others and some of the kids
laugh, it's all right. I know
you're the best and once
you get in the
ground, you'll

be fine. So just don't worry."

No one laughed at Stanley.

When the pots were lined up everyone could see that Stanley had to be taken seriously. Stanley was at least ten centimetres taller than all the other sunflowers, even Jennifer's.

"Ooooooo," said Class 4.

"Did you do that?" said
Mr Prewett.

"Yes," said Ben, just as
surprised as everyone else.

Mr Prewett's nose twitched
and his glasses wobbled. That's

what happened when he didn't believe you, when he thought something not quite right was going on. Ben would have explained about the growing gloves and about talking to Stanley, but he could see that this just wasn't the right time.

Mr Prewett gave everyone a plastic label.

"Write your name, and tie the label to your sunflower."

Ben got out a pencil and wrote his name.

"When we've finished planting," said Mr Prewett, "we can measure the sunflowers and fill in this chart I've made. We'll do that every week until the end of term. And then . . ."

Mr Prewett held up a parcel. It was wrapped in pink-and-silver paper and tied with pink ribbons. "Whoever has grown the biggest sunflower will find out what's inside this parcel."

"Ooooooo," said Class 4.

Ben wasn't sure he wanted a parcel wrapped in pink-and-silver paper, but he knew someone who would.

Outside, Mr Prewett had dug over a patch of dirt by the fence. He had planted some big, strong sticks. Ben looked at the clumps of brown soil. He wished he'd brought Grandad's growing gloves.

When it was his turn, Ben

took a trowel and dug a hole
for Stanley. Next to him, at the
same stick,
Jennifer
Sugden
was
planting
her
sunflower.

Ben felt her eyes slide over his
shoulder. He ignored her,
whispering quietly to Stanley.

"This might be a bit nippy
round the toes."

He tipped up the pot,
exposing Stanley's white roots.

Gently he stood Stanley in the hole and firmed the soil around him.

"Go on," he said. "Have a good stretch."

Ben adjusted the label around Stanley's neck.

"Not too tight, is it?"

When Ben stepped back to admire Stanley, standing so tall and straight, he couldn't help  noticing the pale, droopy specimen Jennifer Sugden was planting. She turned around, scowling.

Her mouth scrunched up small.
"How did you do that?" she
demanded, waving her trowel
very close to Ben's nose.

He might have told
Mr Prewett about the gloves,
and about talking to Stanley,
but he wasn't going to tell
Jennifer.

"Green fingers," he said,
brushing the dirt off his
trousers.

"Who are you kidding?" said Jennifer. "You wait. Mine'll be the biggest. I'll win. Not this weed."

She waved the trowel at Stanley, the edge of the bright metal touching his leaves. Ben gasped. Jennifer's face dissolved into a sneer. She turned and marched back to where Mr Prewett was waiting.

"It's all right," said Ben. "She won't hurt you, Stanley."

# Chapter Three

Put your name next to
your sunflower's height

| | |
|---|---|
| 800 | |
| 790 | |
| 780 | |
| 270 | |
| 260 | |
| 250 | |
| 240 | |
| 230 | |
| 220 | |
| 210 | |
| 200 | |
| 190 | |
| 180 | |
| 170 | |
| 160 | |
| 150 | |
| 140 | |
| 130 | |
| 120 | |
| 110 | |
| 100 | |
| 90 | |
| 80 | |
| 70 | |
| 60 | |
| 50 | Ben |
| 40 | ~~ ~~ |
| 30 | ~~ ~~ ~~ |
| 20 | ~~ ~~ ~~ ~~ ~~ |
| 10 | ~~ ~~ ~~ |

In the classroom Ben recorded
Stanley's height on Mr Prewett's
chart: 50 centimetres. Looking

further down the chart, he could see that no one came near to that. Jennifer Sugden's plant was 35 centimetres.

"Sunflowers," said Mr Prewett, "are unpredictable, a bit like children. They all grow at different speeds. We'll measure them again next week to see how they're getting on."

Every day Ben went to see Stanley for a chat. He didn't

want to tell Stanley but Jennifer had made him feel nervous. His hands felt sticky every time he thought about what she might do. Ben tried to keep calm. He

didn't want Stanley to be afraid.

"How are you doing, Stan? Need a drink?"

"Cowboy mince today, Stan.

Wish I'd brought sandwiches."

"Got all my tables right, Stan."

"Guess what, Stan? Mr Prewett's got the hump."

But sometimes when Ben looked at Stanley he felt so proud he just stood and watched him, growing tall and straight and strong.

Every Monday morning
Class 4 measured their
sunflowers. Mr Prewett was
right. Some of the sunflowers
grew slowly, a centimetre at a

time. Some of them rushed
through six centimetres all at
once and then nothing for a
couple of weeks. Stanley just
grew and grew and grew.

It was bright and sunny on
the last Monday morning. Ben
got up early. On Friday there
had been a bud, and now, at
the top of Stanley's fat, green,
hairy stem was a yellow flower
the size of a dinner plate.

"Brilliomo, Stan," said Ben.

"Brilli-flipping-omo."

All the sunflowers had grown tall. Class 4 needed a stepladder and a long stick to measure the plants. Ben was first. He had to stand right at the top of the ladder

to reach. He went inside to
mark Stanley's new, colossal
height on the chart. He
couldn't help smiling. He'd seen
Jennifer Sugden's sunflower. The
edges of the leaves were yellow
and curly. The stem was bald
and there was no flower.

Later, when everyone had
finished measuring, Ben glanced

down the list. Jennifer Sugden. He couldn't believe what she'd written. Jennifer Sugden's

| 180 cm | Ben. | Jennifer H. Sugden |
|--------|------|--------------------|
| 170 cm |      |                    |

sunflower had shot up in the last week. Really shot up. Her sunflower had shot up so far that it was now the same height as Stanley – exactly.

Ben knew it wasn't true. As soon as the bell went for break, he raced out to see Stanley, just to be sure.

"All right, Stan?" he said, not

wanting Stanley to be worried.
"Everything OK?"

Ben gave Stanley a drink
and went back to the
playground. He was right.

Stanley stood head and
shoulders above the other
sunflowers. There was no way
Jennifer Sugden's came close.
There was no way her
sunflower was going to win.
Stanley was going to win.

## Chapter Four

Mr Prewett took the chart off the wall for the last time.

"Look at this," he said. "We've got some very tall sunflowers."

Ben looked across at Jennifer

Sugden's smiling face and felt
shivery in his tummy.

"Mr Snookley is coming to
see them," said Mr Prewett.
"He'll present the prize in
Assembly later."

Outside, Class 4 waited for
the head teacher to arrive. The
row of sunflowers towered
above their heads. Stanley's
huge, yellow face was turned
up towards the sky. The girls

were crowded around Jennifer,
giggling and talking. None of
the boys seemed interested. Ben

was interested. He stood close
to Stanley, stroking his furry
stem. He knew that Stanley
was the tallest. Everyone could
see it. Now, it did matter who

won, not because Ben wanted
the prize, but
because Stanley

had tried so
hard.
"This is
amazing,"
said Mr
Snookley,
studying
the chart.
"A draw."
"A draw?"
said Ben.
"A draw?" said Mr Prewett.
The girls stopped giggling.

Everyone looked
up at the sunflowers.

Mr
Snookley
looked up at
Stanley and
then back
at the chart.
"This can't
be right,"
he took
hold of
Stanley's
fat, green,
hairy stem and gave it a shake.
"Whose is this?"

"Mine," said Ben – and
Jennifer Sugden.

"Oooooooo," said Class 4.

"I see what's happened," said
Mr Snookley. "They've both
measured the same sunflower,
easily done."

Everyone in Class 4,
especially Ben, knew that it

was not easily done. It could
only have been done on
purpose.

"What have you been up to,
Ben?" said Mr Prewett.

"ME?" said Ben.

"We'll soon sort this out,"
said Mr Prewett, trying to hold
his glasses still while he
searched among the leaves.

"The names are on the labels."

But the labels lay in the dirt. One had been stretched by Stanley's growing stem until it had finally burst and fallen to the ground. The other label had been cut in two. Mr Prewett picked them up. Out in the sun and rain for so many weeks,

they were difficult to read. He rubbed away the dirt with his thumb.

"There's nothing on this one," he said. "But this says 'J', yes, 'J' for Jennifer."

Jennifer Sugden folded her arms and beamed a wide smile.

Ben was gasping for breath.

"It might say 'J' for Jennifer," he said, "but that doesn't make it her sunflower. He's called Stanley. He's the biggest and I grew him, me, not rotten, cheating Jennifer Sugden."

"Ooooo," said Class 4.

"Calm down, now," said Mr Prewett, taking a firm hold of Ben's shoulder.

"I don't want to calm
down," said Ben.

"You've been measuring the
wrong sunflower."

"I haven't," said Ben. He felt
hot. His eyes prickled. "I
promise I haven't. Stanley's my
sunflower. I grew him."

A shadow had filled the
playground as high above their

heads clouds drifted across the
sky. A gentle breeze disturbed
the air as slowly, very slowly,
Stanley's face turned away
from the sun. His stem bent
towards them and in the warm
breeze his head nodded up and
down, up and down.

Ben struggled free. "Look,
look," he shouted. "He's

nodding. Brilliomo, Stan. Brilli-
flipping-omo. You're mine,
aren't you? See, he's mine."

Stanley's petals ruffled Ben's
hair.

"Jennifer," said Mr Prewett. "Is this Ben's sunflower?"

Jennifer's mouth hung open, her eyes wide, staring at Stanley. "Yes," she said, nodding her head up and down, just like Stanley.

"The labels must have got muddled," said Mr Prewett, taking off his glasses.

No one cared about the labels. Everyone was watching as the clouds overhead moved on and Stanley slowly turned his face back towards the sun.

# Chapter Five

Ben had to go on the stage in
Assembly. He'd never, ever had

to do that before.

"Now, young Ben," said Mr Snookley. "To what do you owe your success?"

"Um," Ben didn't know
what to say. "My grandad's got
these . . ."

"Green fingers?" interrupted
Mr Snookley. "I expect you've
inherited them." He handed
Ben the parcel. It was still tied
up with the pink ribbons.

Ben couldn't wait to tell Grandad what Stanley had done.

"Why do you think he's called a sunflower?" said Grandad.

"'Cos his face looks like the sun?"

"Might be," said Grandad.

"But it's also to do with the way their stems grow. The side facing away from the sun grows quicker, so it can get to the light. That's why their faces follow the sun."

"Oh," said Ben.

"Did you think it was magic?" said Grandad.

"No," said Ben. "Course not." He put the parcel on the table. "This is my prize."

"Looks a bit girly to me," said Grandad. "Pink ribbons?"

"They thought Jennifer
would win," said Ben. "They
didn't know about Stanley."

Inside the parcel was a
trowel, a little fork and some
gardening gloves.

"Swap you?" said Ben.

"Not likely," said Grandad.

There was a book about
gardening and some packets of
seeds.

"We're going to be busy,"
said Ben, tearing open one of

the packets. "What's a good name for a lupin?"

"Lionel?"

"Don't be daft."

"What about . . ." Grandad stopped. "What do you mean *we're* going to be busy?"

"There's hundreds of these lupins," said Ben. "And there's all these pansies and petunias. What's a good name for a salvia?"

Grandad rubbed his chin.

"Stanley?" he said.

"Stanley?" said Ben. "There'll only ever be one Stanley – Stanley Sunflower, the biggest and the best."

THE END

# BLACK ADAM
## AND THE
# ETERNITY WAR

BY
DEREK FRIDOLFS

ILLUSTRATED BY
TIM LEVINS

raintree

a Capstone company—publishers for children

Published by Raintree, an imprint of Capstone Global Library Limited,
a company incorporated in England and Wales having its registered
office at 264 Banbury Road, Oxford, OX2 7DY – Registered company
number: 6695582

www.raintree.co.uk
myorders@raintree.co.uk

STAR40491

ISBN 978 1 4747 5481 1
22 21 20 19 18
10 9 8 7 6 5 4 3 2 1

A full catalogue record for this book is available from the British Library.

Editor: Christopher Harbo
Designer: Bob Lentz

Printed and bound in India.